ISBN: 0-7172-8787-4

Based on the Pooh stories by A.A. Milne
(copyright The Pooh Properties Trust).

Based on the Direct to Video
Pooh's Grand Adventure: The Search For Christopher Robin
written by Karl Geurs and Carter Crocker

Story Adapted by Catherine McCafferty
Illustrated by John Kurtz

DISNEP'S
POOH'S GRAND
ADVENTURE
The Search For Christopher Robin

GROLIER
B O O K S

*O*nce upon the last day of a golden summer...

...there was a boy and a bear. And together
they had many grand adventures in a remarkable
place called the Hundred-Acre Wood.

But the grandest and most extraordinary
of all their adventures was still to begin.
The bear did not know it, but a great
change was coming. His very best friend
was about to leave.

Winnie the Pooh hummed a happy hum as Christopher Robin came to see him. Pooh didn't know that Christopher Robin would start school the next day. And Pooh didn't want to listen as Christopher Robin talked about good byes.

Hellos were much happier things to Pooh. "You're just in time for the best part of the day," Pooh told his friend, "the part when you and me become we."

And so Pooh led
Christopher Robin
on a day
full of play.

At the end of the last day of that golden summer, Christopher Robin tried again to say good-bye. "Pooh Bear," he said, "if there's ever a tomorrow when we're not together, there's something you must remember:

You're braver than you believe, and stronger than you seem, and smarter than you think."

Pooh Bear was sleepy from his hard day at play. He mixed up the words as he tried to repeat them. And he drifted off to sleep as Christopher Robin added, "But the most important thing is, even if we're apart, I'll always be with you."

The very next day, the first crisp day of autumn came to the Hundred-Acre Wood. Long before Pooh awoke, Christopher Robin left a pot of honey outside Pooh's door. He stuck a note to it, telling Pooh he was going to school. And then he went away.

Later that morning, Pooh found the honey. Honey was for eating, thought Pooh, but was this honey his to eat? He got so stuck on the question that he didn't even see Christopher Robin's note.

Pooh decided to ask Christopher Robin about the honey. But when he went looking for his friend at Piglet's house, Pooh found only Piglet, high in a tree. "I'm doing what Christopher Robin said I should do," Piglet called. "I'm conquering my fear of heights."

Piglet's fear returned, though, when his branch cracked under him.

"Hoo-hoo-hoo!" Tigger bounced in, all ready to save Piglet. But Tigger's tail wouldn't bounce him all the way up. All Tigger could do was catch Piglet on the way down.

An avalanche of acorns from Piglet's tree sent the
friends rolling toward Rabbit's house.

Now, Rabbit was not expecting company. His garden
book said it was Harvest Day. "Even if you think you're
not ripe," he told his plants, "we go by the book!"

But before he could pick a single pea, he was swept
toward Eeyore's house of twigs!

The tumble of Tigger and Piglet and Rabbit and Pooh left Eeyore without even one twig over his head. When they had rolled to a rest, Pooh showed everyone the honeypot. "If I could find Christopher Robin," Pooh said "he could tell me whose honey this is."

"Why don't we check the note?" Rabbit asked.

Now, a note with writing meant a visit to Owl's house. Owl studied the note carefully, then read it out loud: "Worry about me. I'm going far away. Help. Christopher Robin." Owl saw that Christopher Robin said he was going to "s-c-h-o-o-l." To Owl's eyes, that spelled "skull."

And that, Owl added, spelled danger for their friend. "We must help him get back here!" Pooh said.

"Ah!" said Owl. "You're going on a quest!" He drew
a map and told them of the terrible Skullasaurus they
would meet. "You must go to the Forbidden Mountains,
then find the Eye of the Skull to save Christopher Robin,"
he warned them.

By the time Owl sent them on their way, even Pooh
was trembly.

Pooh and his friends followed Owl's map through the Woods, then the Bigger Woods, then the Much Bigger Woods, until they came to the Upside-Down Rock.

"If you're here, you're where the monsters are," Rabbit read over Pooh's shoulder. Sure enough, they heard a loud growl nearby!

"The Skullasaurus!" yelped Piglet.

But Rabbit wasn't rattled. They had a map to follow, after all. And a map was as good as a book for telling them what to do. Rabbit took the map from Pooh. With one quick I-know-what-I'm-doing look at it, he pointed them in the direction he thought was right.

"No Skullasaurus would dare follow us in here," Rabbit told the others.

But a moment later, they heard another growl. Piglet raced off in a panic—and found a beautiful meadow! Some friendly butterflies tickled Piglet. Then they carried him away!

Pooh tried to help his frightened friend. "You're bigger than a big leaf!" he shouted to Piglet, mixing up Christopher Robin's words about being braver than you believe. That didn't help, so Pooh jumped up and grabbed him by the leg. That did help, sort of. The butterflies couldn't lift Pooh and Piglet, so they both came back to earth with a crash!

"That was very brave of you, Pooh," said Piglet.

"You're brave, too, Piglet," Pooh answered. "Braver than...something. Er, Rabbit," Pooh asked, "are those the mountains we're looking for?"

Pooh trusted his eyes. Rabbit trusted the map—until the wind grabbed the map away.

The map hovered near a deep gorge. Tigger ran out onto a log and began to bounce up to grab it. He bounced ...and he bounced...and he bounced, but he couldn't reach the map. "What's causing this tail to fail?" he moaned. He made one more bounce—and the log cracked beneath him.

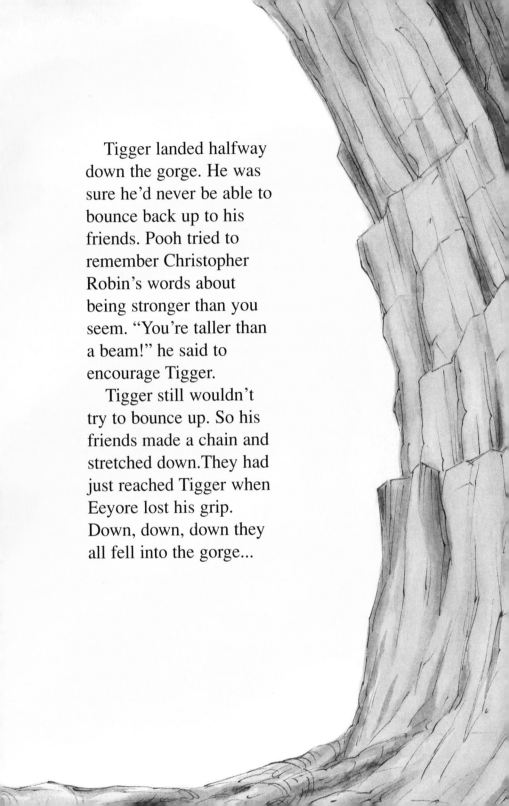

Tigger landed halfway down the gorge. He was sure he'd never be able to bounce back up to his friends. Pooh tried to remember Christopher Robin's words about being stronger than you seem. "You're taller than a beam!" he said to encourage Tigger.

Tigger still wouldn't try to bounce up. So his friends made a chain and stretched down. They had just reached Tigger when Eeyore lost his grip. Down, down, down they all fell into the gorge...

...until they landed with a muddy splat! The map floated down through the mist and landed, too—on Rabbit's head.

"Might you know which way Christopher Robin is from here, Rabbit?" Pooh asked hopefully.

Rabbit just shook his head. "I am not smart enough to know," he said.

Pooh tried to remember Christopher Robin's words about being smarter than you think. "You're smarter when you're pink," Pooh told Rabbit.

Rabbit still felt that he had failed. All of them felt lost and alone and wished that Christopher Robin was there. Discouraged, they went to a cave to wait for the mist to clear.

When the mist stopped being so misty, Piglet discovered that their cave was Skull Cave! They had to find a way to reach Christopher Robin in the Eye of the Skull! But as the growl of the Skullasaurus echoed around them, all they found was a crystal cavern.

When the friends heard another growl, they ran! But Pooh slipped and got stuck behind a crystal block. With his face squashed against the clear block, he could see his friends, but he couldn't call to them. His friends thought that the Skullasaurus had gobbled Pooh up! How could they reach the Eye of the Skull without Pooh?

Then Rabbit surprised himself by getting an idea:
Tigger could bounce Piglet up to the Eye.

Tigger surprised himself by making the bounce.

Then Piglet surprised himself by being brave enough
to stand on the high ledge and lower a vine so the others
could climb up to the Eye!

Pooh had seen the whole thing. But just as his friends
got up to him, Pooh came unstuck and slid down, down,
deep into the cave.

All alone, Pooh thought of Christopher Robin and remembered his friend's true words. "Piglet was so much braver than he believes," said Pooh. "And Tigger was stronger than he seems. And Rabbit, smarter than he thinks!"

Then Pooh remembered Christopher Robin saying, "Even if we're apart, I'll always be with you." Suddenly, Pooh didn't feel so alone anymore.

Far from Pooh, his friends huddled together.
Something was moving closer to them in the cave.
It was...Christopher Robin!
   "Where have you been?" he asked.

"We had to save you from Skull," Tigger said.
"Skull?" said Christopher Robin. "I've been
at *school*."

The others explained about the map and the quest. Christopher Robin explained what Owl had missed in his note: "Don't worry" and "I'm not going far away" and "Help yourself to the honey." Honey reminded Christopher Robin of Pooh. "Where is Pooh?" he asked.

A growl sounded deep in the cave as Piglet sadly said, "In there. The Skullasaurus gobbled him up!"

But Christopher Robin was not sad at all. "That's no Skullasaurus," he said. "That's the sound of the rumbly tumbly of a hungry-for-honey Pooh Bear!"

Faster than you could say "honeypot," Christopher Robin made a rescue plan. He tied a Pooh-sized honeypot to a rope and lowered it to where Pooh was sitting with his smackerel-sized honeypot. When Pooh saw the big honeypot, he got into it. Christopher Robin pulled him right up.

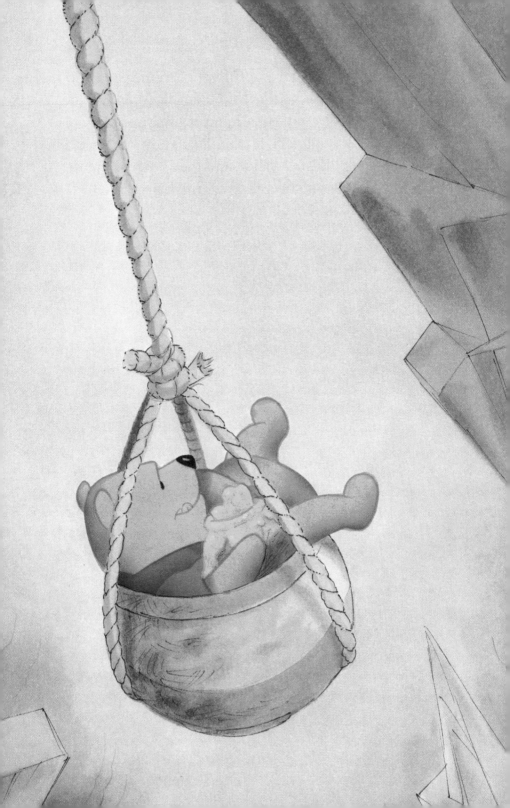

There was no happier Pooh Bear than the one who hugged Christopher Robin. And there were no happier friends than Piglet and Tigger and Rabbit and Eeyore when they saw Pooh safe and sound. They had found their friends—and they had found their own strengths.

Their quest was a success, two times over.

Later, Christopher Robin told Pooh about school.
"I learn things there. It was scary at first. But when
I found myself feeling alone, I thought of you, Pooh."

"That's what I would have done," Pooh said.

"Pooh?" Christopher Robin said. "Promise you won't
forget about me?"

"I promise," said Pooh.

"And you'll remember that even if we're apart, I'll
always be with you?"

"Yes, Christopher Robin," answered Pooh. "And I
shall always be with you."